Developing Reader titles are ideal for using their phonics knowledge and ca... with only a little help. Frequently repeated words help improve fluency and confidence.

Special features:

Short, simple sentences

Frequent repetition of main story words and phrases

Careful match between story and pictures

Large, clear type

Ladybird

Educational Consultant: James Clements
Autism Consultant: Child Autism UK
Cerebral Palsy Consultant: Pace
Book Banding Consultant: Kate Ruttle

LADYBIRD BOOKS

UK | USA | Canada | Ireland | Australia
India | New Zealand | South Africa

Ladybird Books is part of the Penguin Random House group of companies whose addresses can be found at global.penguinrandomhouse.com.

www.penguin.co.uk   www.puffin.co.uk   www.ladybird.co.uk

First published 2024
001

Written by Claire Smith
Text copyright © Ladybird Books Ltd, 2024
Illustrations by Martyn Cain
Illustrations copyright © Ladybird Books Ltd, 2024

The moral right of the illustrator has been asserted

Printed in China

The authorized representative in the EEA is Penguin Random House Ireland, Morrison Chambers, 32 Nassau Street, Dublin D02 YH68

A CIP catalogue record for this book is available from the British Library

ISBN: 978-0-241-56393-9

All correspondence to:
Ladybird Books
Penguin Random House Children's
One Embassy Gardens, 8 Viaduct Gardens, London SW11 7BW

The Video Game

Written by Claire Smith
Illustrated by Martyn Cain

Miss Zebra had a new video-game book.

"The video game is Zap Land," said Miss Zebra.

"I love playing video games with all my friends," said Nia Hedgehog.

"This is a new game!" said Noah Panda. "What can we do in Zap Land?"

"You can make buildings and you can win treasure," said Miss Zebra.

"And here we are," said Miss Zebra. "You can make buildings with these blocks."

"Here are some buttons," said Nia. "We can push them to move the blocks up, down, left or right. We can make a house."

"This is a great house!" said Miss Zebra.

"Everyone can go in the house and play," said Nia.

"There is no treasure here," said Noah. "Where is it?"

"Look at the wizards!" said Noah.

"We will pull down your house!" said the wizards.

"Oh no!" said Nia.

But Nia had flowers. "I can throw flowers at the wizards!" said Nia. "Wizards do not like flowers!"

"Everyone throw flowers at the wizards!" said Noah.

"The wizards are going now!" said Nia.

"You can make more buildings with these blocks," said Miss Zebra.

"Here are more buttons," said Nia. "We can push them to move the blocks up, down, left or right. We can make a castle."

"What a great castle!"
said Miss Zebra.

"Everyone can go in the castle and play," said Nia.

"There is no treasure here," said Noah. "Where is it?"

"Look at the witches!" said Noah.

"Now we will pull down your castle!" said the witches.

"Oh no!" said Nia.

But Noah had cupcakes.
"I can throw cupcakes at the witches!" said Noah. "Witches do not like cupcakes!"

"Everyone throw cupcakes at the witches!" said Nia.

"The witches are going now!" said Nia.

"Look!" said Noah. "There is some treasure here now!"

"We win the treasure, and we win the game!" said Nia.

"Great game, everyone!" said Miss Zebra.

"I love this book and I love playing Zap Land with all my friends!" said Noah.

How much do you remember about the story of *The Video Game*? Answer these questions and find out!

- How can the friends make the blocks move?

- How does everyone make the wizards go away?

- How does everyone make the witches go away?

- How do the friends win the game?